This Book Belongs to

_____

ZONDERKIDZ

Believe Coloring Book
Text copyright © 2015 by Randy Frazee
Illustrations copyright © 2015 by Macky Pamintuan

Requests for information should be addressed to:

Zonderkidz, 3900 *Sparks Drive SE, Grand Rapids, Michigan* 49546

ISBN 978-0-310-75222-6

Design: Cindy Davis

Printed in the United States of America

15 16 17 18 19 /PHP/ 11 10 9 8 7 6 5 4 3

BELIEVE

COLORING BOOK

THINK, ACT, BE LIKE JESUS

God's Wonderful Creation: *Genesis 1–2*

Key Idea: I believe the God of the Bible is the only true God—Father, Son, and Holy Spirit.

The Baptism of Jesus: *Luke 3*
Key Verse: May the love that God has given us be with you.
—*2 Corinthians 13:14*

The Lord Is My Shepherd: *Psalm 23*
Key Idea: I believe God is involved in and cares about my daily life.

Why Worry?: *Matthew 6:25–34*

Key Verse: My help comes from the LORD. He is the Maker of heaven and earth.

—*Psalm 121:2*

Adam and Eve Disobey God: *Genesis 2–3*
Key Idea: I believe a person can have a relationship with
God by God's grace through faith in Jesus Christ.

He is Risen!: *Luke 24:1–12*
Key Verse: God's grace has saved you because of your faith in Christ.
—*Ephesians 2:8*

Rules to Live By: *Exodus 20:1–17*

Key Idea: I believe the Bible is God's Word and it guides my beliefs and actions.

Jesus Is Tempted: *Matthew 4:1–11*
Key Verse: God has breathed life into all Scripture. It is useful for teaching us what is true.
—2 Timothy 3:16

God Changes Abram's and Sarai's Names: *Genesis 12:1–8; 17:1–7, 15–17*
Key Idea: I believe I am significant because I am a child of God.

The Change in Zacchaeus: *Luke 19:1–10*
Key Verse: Some people did accept him and did believe in his name.
He gave them the right to become children of God. —*John 1:12*

God Builds a Nation: *Genesis 15:1–7; 17:15–22; 18:10–15; 21:1–7*

Key Idea: I believe God uses the church to bring about his plan.

The Holy Spirit Comes to Establish the Church: *Acts 2:1–14*
Key Verse: We will speak the truth in love. So we will grow up in
every way to become the body of Christ. *—Ephesians 4:15*

Cain and Abel: *Genesis 4:1–16*
Key Idea: I believe all people are loved by God and need Jesus Christ as their Savior.

The Lost Sheep Is Found: *Matthew 18:10–14*
Key Verse: God so loved the world that he gave his one and only Son.
Anyone who believes in him will not die but will have eternal life. —*John 3:16*

Ruth and Boaz: *Ruth 1–4*

Key Idea: I believe God calls all Christians to show compassion to people in need.

The Good Samaritan: *Luke 10:25–37*
Key Verse: Save those who are weak and needy.
—Psalm 82:4

Hannah and Samuel: *1 Samuel 1:1–28, 3:1–11*

Key Idea: I believe everything I am and everything I own belong to God.

A Widow's Gift: *Mark 12:38–44*

Key Verse: The earth belongs to the LORD. And so does everything in it.

—*Psalm 24:1*

Elijah Goes to Heaven: *2 Kings 2:1–17*
Key Idea: I believe there is a heaven and a hell and that
Jesus will return to establish his eternal kingdom.

John's Vision of Heaven: *Revelation 4:1–8; 7:9; 21:11–22*
Key Verse: Do not let your hearts be troubled ... There are many rooms in my Father's house.
—*John 14:1–2*

Daniel Only Worships God: *Daniel 6*
Key Idea: I worship God for who he is and what he has done for me.

Paul and Silas Worship God in Prison: *Act 16:16–35*

Key Verse: Come, let us sing for joy to the Lord.

Let us give a loud shout to the Rock who saves us. —*Psalm 95:1*

Gideon Talks to God: *Judges 6–7*

Key Idea: I pray to God to know him and find direction in my life.

Jesus Teaches His Disciples to Pray: *Luke 11:1–12*
Key Verse: God has surely listened. He has heard my prayer ...
He has not held back his love from me. —*Psalm 66:19–20*

God Tells Joshua to Remember the Law: *Joshua 1:1–11*

Key Idea: I study the Bible to know God and his truth and to find direction for my daily life.

Jesus Teaches About Four Kinds of Soil: *Matthew 13:1– 23*

Key Verse: The word of God is alive and active.

—*Hebrews 4:12*

Jehoshaphat Prays to God for Help: *2 Chronicles 20:1–30*
Key Idea: I focus on God and his priorities for my life.

Jesus Walks on Water: *Matthew 14:22–32*
Key Verse: Put God's kingdom first. Do what he wants you to do.
Then all those things will also be given to you. —*Matthew 6:33*

The Fiery Furnace: *Daniel 3*
Key Idea: I dedicate my life to God's plan.

Stephen's Story: *Acts 6:8–7:60*
Key Verse: When you offer your bodies to God, you are
worshiping him in the right way. —*Romans 12:1*

Rebuilding the Wall of Jerusalem: *Nehemiah 2:11–4:23; 6:15*
Key Idea: I spend time with other Christians to accomplish God's
plan in my life, in the lives of others, and in the world.

A Community of Believers: *Acts 2:42–47; 4:32–37*

Key Verse: All the believers were together. They shared everything they had.

—*Acts 2:44*

Daniel Interprets the King's Dream: *Daniel 2:1–47*
Key Idea: I know my spiritual gifts and use them to bring about God's plan.

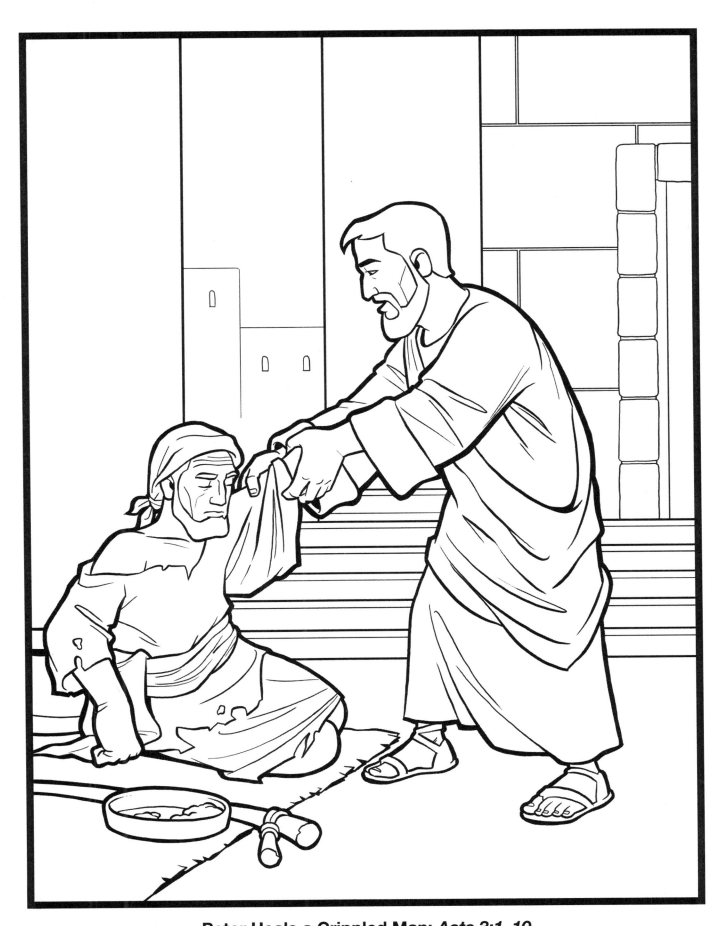

Peter Heals a Crippled Man: *Acts 3:1–10*
Key Verse: We all have gifts. They differ according to the grace
God has given to each of us. —*Romans 12:6*

God's People Finish Building the Temple: *Haggai 1:1–15*
Key Idea: I offer my time to help God's plan.

Jesus in His Father's House: *Luke 2:41–52*
Key Verse: Do everything you say or do in the name of the Lord Jesus.
—*Colossians 3:17*

Gifts for the Tabernacle: *Exodus 35:4–29; 36:1–6*
Key Idea: I give my resources to help God's plan.

The Wise Men Visit Jesus: *Matthew 2:1–15*
Key Verse: Make sure that you also do well in the grace of giving to others.
—*2 Corinthians 8:7*

Jonah Tells Other People About God: *Jonah 1–4*
Key Idea: I share my faith with others to help God's plan.

Philip Shares the Bible with a Man from Ethiopia: *Acts 8:26–40*

Key Verse: So pray that I will be bold as I preach the good news.
—Ephesians 6:20

David and Jonathan: *1 Samuel 18:1–4; 19:1–7; 20:1–42*
Key Idea: I will try hard to love God and love others.

A Good Shepherd Loves His Sheep: *John 10:14–18*
Key Verse: Since God loved us this much, we should also love one another.
—1 John 4:11

Celebrating the Joy of the Lord: *Nehemiah 8:13–17*

Key Idea: No matter what happens, I feel happy inside and understand God's plan for my life.

Angels Give the Shepherds Joyful News: *Luke 2:1–20*
Key Verse: I have told you this so that you will have the same joy that I have.
—John 15:11

Solomon's Kingdom at Peace: *1 Kings 3:1–15; 4:20–25*
Key Idea: I am not worried. I have found peace with God,
peace with others, and peace with myself.

Jesus Calms the Storm: *Mark 4:35–41*
Key Verse: Don't worry about anything ... God's peace will watch
over your hearts and your minds. —*Philippians 4:6—7*

Samson Loses Control: *Judges 13–16*
Key Idea: I have the power through Jesus to control myself.

The Lost Son: *Luke 15:11–32*

Key Verse: We must control ourselves. We must do what is right.

—*Titus 2:12*

Isaiah the Prophet Brings Hope: *Isaiah 40*

Key Idea: I can deal with the hardships of life because of the hope I have in Jesus.

Simeon's Story: *Luke 2:22–35*
Key Verse: Our hope is certain ... It is strong and secure.
—*Hebrews 6:19*

David's Patience with King Saul: *1 Samuel 24:1–22*

Key Idea: I do not get angry quickly, and I am patient, even when things go wrong.

Jesus Heals a Disabled Man: *John 5:1–15*
Key Verse: Anyone who is patient has great understanding.
—*Proverbs 14:29*

David Shows Kindness to Jonathan's Son: *2 Samuel 9:1–13; 16:1–4; 19:24–30*
Key Idea: I choose to be kind and good in my relationships with others.

Jesus Talks about Kindness: *Luke 14:1–14*

Key Verse: Always try to do what is good for each other and for everyone else.

—1 Thessalonians 5:15

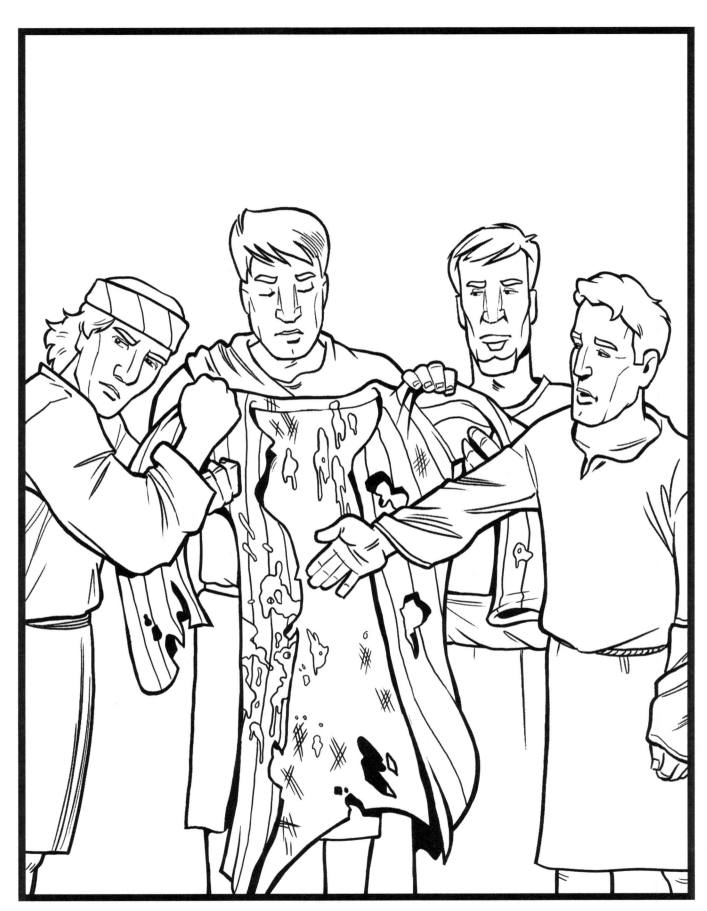

God and Joseph—Faithful to One Another: *Genesis 37–46*
Key Idea: I can be trusted because I keep my promises to God and others.

The Angel's Visit: *Luke 1:26–38*

Key Verse: Lord, your faithful love reaches up to the skies.
—Psalm 36:5

Abigail Is Gentle with David: *1 Samuel 25*
Key Idea: I am thoughtful, considerate, and calm with others.

Jesus Gently Questions Peter: *John 21*
Key Verse: Let everyone know how gentle you are.
—*Philippians 4:5*

God Humbles a Proud King: *Daniel 4:1–37*
Key Idea: I choose to value others more than myself.

Jesus Humbles Himself in Front of His Disciples: *John 13:1–17*
Key Verse: Value others more than yourselves.
—*Philippians 2:3*